This 1988 edition published by Derrydale Books,
distributed by Crown Publishers, Inc
225 Park Avenue South, New York,
New York 10003.

ISBN - 0-517-66272-8

h g f e d c b a

THE BEST BEDTIME STORIES

OF MOTHER CAT

Stories by Anne-Marie Dalmais
illustrated by Violayne Hulné

English translation by DIANE COHEN

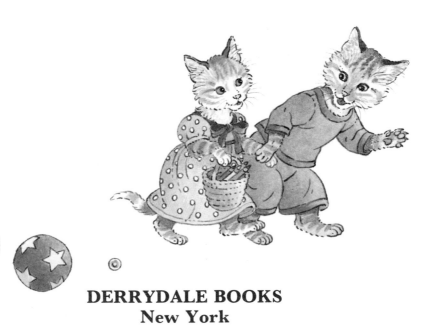

DERRYDALE BOOKS
New York

6

Yes, it's a rocket — a *paper* rocket, thin, long and streamlined — that brushes the tips of Mother Cat's ears when she walks into the bedroom where her kittens are playing. Of course the rocket wasn't meant to hit her — but Mother Cat opened the door at the exact moment it was tossed into the air.

Luckily for her, she ducked just in time!

These kittens have turned their room completely topsy-turvy! Her two little sons have built an entire fleet of missiles that they launch one by one: Zoom! Zoom!! Zoom!!! They fling the paper rockets in all directions.

One kitten climbs up on his brother's shoulders to throw the missiles higher and higher.

Two of their sisters are doing all sorts of tricks, and they are playing badminton on top of their beds. The baby girl, angry with being left out, is having a tantrum. Then, one after the other, the five kittens sing:

"Straight in the bull's eye,
See my rocket fly!"
the little boys chant.
"First you whack it,
Then I smack it."

"Badminton's our favorite game!"
the little girls add.
"One and two make three,
Who will play with me?"
asks the baby, still sobbing.

"Well, this is a shame," their mother says. "I've come at a bad time. I wanted to tell you a story, maybe even two, but in this mess and with your running around, I see that it's impossible."

The kittens won't hear of this. They *really* want to hear a story. So, believe it or not, before you can say "Abracadabra," the room is cleaned up and our five little kittens have become as good as gold.

An Ocean Liner Voyage

Once upon a time there was a family of eccentric cats: the Hurly-Burlies — not your run-of-the-mill, stay-at-home, quiet cat family, mind you!

The father, whose name was Basil, adored traveling. The mother, called Periwinkle, shared his wanderlust and followed her husband with a great deal of enthusiasm... and a great deal of luggage! Their daughters, Hawthorn and Wildrose, thought this whirlwind life was very entertaining.

Running here and there, they were restless, quick-witted and lively as fireflies — sometimes just a little too lively. Suddenly they would become moody, spoiled, and even a little bit spiteful — like two pretty flowers with thorns.

This morning at home with the Hurly-Burlies is no ordinary morning.

The entire family is sailing to Europe aboard an ocean liner — imagine that!

What a great day!

Of course, our friends the cats are accustomed to traveling. But each time is a new adventure. There is endless shouting and yelling and total confusion — what pandemonium!

For the umpteenth time, Mr. Hurly-Burly counts the pieces of luggage — the suitcases and bags, that is, because, luckily, the trunks were sent the day before. (They will cross the ocean down in the ship's hold.)

Even so, several packages are left and each time Mr. Hurly-Burly counts them, in his haste, he comes up with a different number.

"It's witchcraft!" he moans, while Mrs. Hurly-Burly asks him, also for the umpteenth time:

"Basil, Basil, do you have the tickets?"

"Of course I do, Periwinkle dear, of course I have the tickets!" he answers.

The Hurly-Burlies have to go up and down the stairs several times to bring down this load. Hurray! At last they've done it. Everything is accounted for and family and baggage are lined up at the front door. Suddenly, Hawthorn lets out a piercing scream:

"My doll! I can't leave her here all by herself!"

Mr. Hurly-Burly is kind enough to go back upstairs, reopen padlocks, bolts, and chains, and turn everything upside-down to find her ragdoll kitten.

11

The Hurly-Burlies need two taxis — this shouldn't surprise you — to transport them and all their things. They travel in two speedy yellow cars that follow one another and wind their way through the congested New York City streets.

One last time, Mrs. Hurly-Burly asks her husband,

"Basil, Basil, do you have the tickets?"

And one last time, Mr. Hurly-Burly tells his wife,

"Of course, Periwinkle dear, of course I have the tickets!"

After countless red lights, our travelers finally arrive at the pier.

They receive a friendly greeting from a Badger in a spiffy uniform.

"Good day, Madam! Good day, Sir! And you too, young ladies, good day! May I please see your tickets?"

Oh no! Can it be?

Yes, it's true! Mr. Hurly-Burly suddenly realizes he doesn't have— no definitely not...he doesn't have the tickets!

The Hurly-Burlies panic. What are they going to do now? There's only one solution — to return home!

Mr. Hurly-Burly will go alone and his family will wait for him at the pier. The two little girls are so upset, they start to cry.

13

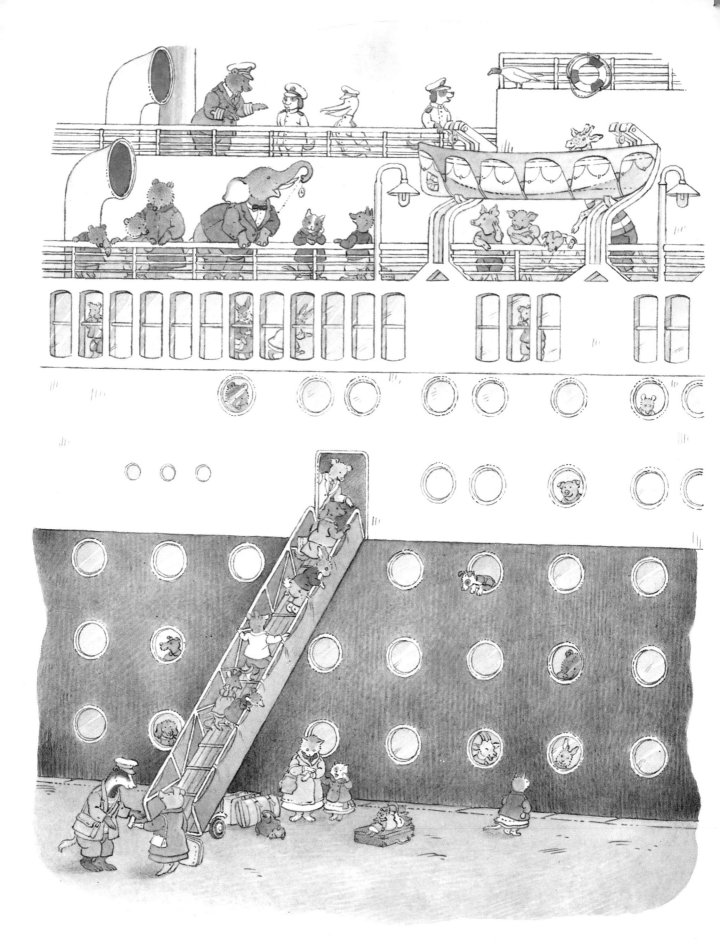

"We're - go - ing to miss - the - boat!" Wildrose hiccups.

"We'll be left behind!" Hawthorn sobs.

The kittens are very distraught. They carry on, rubbing their eyes, sniffling, and coughing. What a scene!

Indeed, it's sad to be at the foot of the gangplank and not be able to go on board this beautiful ship.

And it's annoying to see the other passengers calmly hand over their tickets to Mr. Badger and then, smiling, climb the magic ladder.

Mrs. Hurly-Burly doesn't notice anything because she has her eyes glued to her watch. She can't stop looking at the two hands, going round and round, much too fast for her. "What can Basil be doing?" she mutters, at the end of her rope!

This waiting is irritating; it's exasperating; it's driving her crazy!

After twenty minutes Wildrose gets tired of crying and starts doing balancing tricks at the edge of the dock, when suddenly, the ship's whistle blasts!

At the same moment, Mr. Hurly-Burly appears, running out of breath, but waving the precious tickets!

And just in time too: the Hurly-Burlies only have a few seconds to board the ship!

15

Finally, they're on board!

Mr. Hurly-Burly catches his breath, Mrs. Hurly-Burly calms down, and the two little girls are their smiling selves again.

The beginning of the afternoon is very busy.
They must find their cabin, put away the suitcases and, by order of the captain, carefully practice the life-saving drill.

But then, at last, it's time to play.

Wildrose and Hawthorn happily stroll about the bridge which seems to pitch and dance just for them!

With each passing hour, the fun increases.

And it's one surprise after another for the two kittens. A scrumptious dinner is served, with much fuss, in a dining room where the lights on the ceiling shine like stars.

Then it's time for bed.

What a welcome change to return to a tranquil, cozy cabin after all the mishaps and excitement of the day. What a wonderful feeling to stretch out on a bunkbed with smooth sheets and be rocked to sleep by the rolling waves and the song of the ocean.

And while night is falling, how marvelous to dream about this fabulous journey toward the Old World...

A Stormy Night

Once upon a time there was a little cat who loved to hammer nails. Yes, nails — small, sharp, and pointy ones, by the tens, by the dozens, by the hundreds — all sorts of nails. Everywhere he went he carried his beloved toolbox and, every chance he could find — tap-tap-tap — with a solid blow of his hammer, he drove in, here and there, one of his precious nails! This kitten, whose name was Handy-Andy, liked to do any kind of odd job: sawing, sandpapering, polishing — you name it, he could repair anything.

This afternoon, Handy-Andy is meeting his friend Harry the Hare to help him finish building his cabin.
For more than a month, the two have been constructing this little house. Take a look at the solidly cemented stone foundations, the walls made from wooden boards, perfectly nailed together, and this slanted rooftop, which looks just like a pointed hat.

The cabin still needs a well-fitted door, one that opens and closes easily, a sturdy door, that will keep out bad weather and darkness.

Handy-Andy is doing exactly what he loves to do: tap-tap-tap! He attaches extra bars to make the frame strong.

He hammers in rhythm and hammers in time:
One nail, two nails, three nails, four,
To make it strong, I'll add some more.
Five nails, six nails, seven nails, eight,
This cabin is really looking great!

Meanwhile, Harry the Hare paints the shutters and goes over them several times with his brush.

"Painting sure —
is lots of fun!
Put a dab over there,
And over here a dash.
But do be careful
not to splash!"

As soon as the door is finished, the two friends pick it up, heave-ho, heave-ho, carry it to where it belongs, and try to hang it on its hinges. Phew, is it heavy! They must try again and again. They toil, they sweat, they sigh. Sometimes handiwork requires hard work and perseverance. So, let's give it another go. Hurray! They finally do it. The door is in place — and it works! Now the only thing left is to attach the shutters — the ones that are dry, of course.

The next day, the cabin is practically finished. Their mothers, Mrs. Tall-Ears and Mrs. Sugar-Puss, have announced their arrival. They are both very curious to visit this construction. They've been hearing about it for more than a month. Of course, Mrs. Tall-Ears and Mrs. Sugar-Puss have seen it taking shape from afar, with the walls climbing higher each day and the cabin's frame growing little by little, but this is the first time they're actually on the building site to inspect the work.

They are amazed and utter ohs! and ahs! of delight.

"What an accomplishment!" Mrs. Sugar-Puss exclaims.

"It's a real house! says Mrs. Tall-Ears, ecstatic.

"You could live in it, if you like."

With endless enthusiasm, the two visitors discover the charming details, clever finishing touches, and all the little practical inventions that make the cabin cheerful, inviting, and comfortable.

They are very proud of their children. "They are just like real builders," they say to themselves.

Mrs. Sugar-Puss and Mrs. Tall-Ears compliment Handy-Andy and Harry the Hare over and over for a job well done and then give them their gifts. Each has brought a surprise.

Mrs. Tall-Ears presents them with a small bamboo table — the perfect thing to furnish the first floor. It is just what they need for serving snacks, or for playing cards.

Mrs. Sugar-Puss has chosen two woolen blankets that will cozily cover the wooden beds upstairs.

Harry and Handy-Andy are so happy! Well, wouldn't you be, too? Their mothers kiss and congratulate them again and then return home.

Not long after, another visitor arrives — Sweet-Tooth, the field mouse.

The hare and the kitten welcome him with shouts of joy — especially since this friendly neighbor hasn't come alone, but accompanied by a big wicker basket filled with delicious treats: three huge slices of chocolate cake, glazed apricots, a dozen almond cookies, and a jug of lemonade... a lip-smacking feast.

23

But, suddenly, a terrible hurricane lets loose!

Handy-Andy and Harry are so wrapped up in showing their friend around their home that they didn't notice the sky gradually darken and then quickly become heavy with menacing clouds. The first streak of lightning blinds them and the loud crash of thunder that follows makes them all jump!

A furious wind immediately starts to blow, shaking everything in its path. Our three friends struggle to close their shutters as they battle the gusts of wind. They pull and they tug and finally manage to secure the wooden panels. Quickly, they fasten the hooks. Phew! Here they are barricaded in their cabin, and just in time because the storm is getting worse and the rain now comes beating down on their little house.

"Maybe we should eat," suggests Sweet-Tooth. The hurricane hasn't taken away his appetite one bit.

"First let me turn on a flashlight." Handy-Andy says.

"We can't see a thing anymore!"

"Do you think our house will hold up?" asks Harry the Hare, slightly worried.

And the kitten promptly answers, "No storm will be able to pull out the nails that I hammered! Come on, let's eat."

For the time being, the scrumptious pastries make them forget the lightning and thunder.

But the rumbling noises are coming closer and faster.
It's impossible to leave the cabin — absolutely impossible!
So, the three friends decide to spend the night in the cabin.

Sweet-Tooth the field mouse will sleep downstairs on the bench and use a cushion for a mattress.

"You're sure you don't mind staying down here alone?" his friends ask.

"No, not at all." the field mouse answers. "Anyway, you won't be very far away."

"Good night, Handy-Andy. Good night, Harry."

Sweet-Tooth stretches out comfortably on his pillow, closes his eyes, and thinks about his present situation with satisfaction. He has just eaten a delicious snack, he is living a completely unexpected adventure with his two best friends, and this cabin is like a magical refuge to him. Even the wind's howling becomes a lullaby to his ears. Sweet-Tooth falls asleep, smiling.

26

Upstairs, in the attic, the hare and kitten happily try out their beds and blankets.

Since they're under the rafters, they hear the rain running off the roof just above their heads and the hailstones hammering the boards, jumping and bouncing. The storm rages nonstop.

"I was right to hammer a lot nails!" Handy-Andy congratulates himself. "Double ration! Triple ration! Thanks to that, I'm sure the roof won't blow off!"

Despite the howling wind, the two friends fall fast asleep.

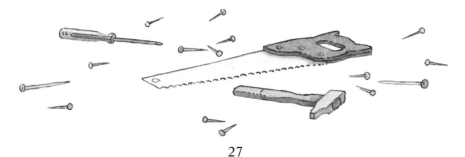

27

But now, back in the bedroom ot the five brothers and sisters —
what's going on there?

Oh! Ssh, ssh! All the kittens are in bed and seem to be sleeping.

They have huddled underneath their sheets as if they, too, wanted to take shelter from the awful hurricane.

Did they even hear the end of the story?

"I would be surprised..." Mother Cat says to herself, amused. "I'll tell it to them another time."

Judging from their peaceful little faces and their calm and tranquil breathing, she suspects they've all gone off to the land of dreams. And by no means would she disturb their mysterious journey into the deep of the night.

Mother Cat watches them tenderly a few moments and then, ever so softly, leaves the room on her velvet paws...